The Amazing Animal Alphabet Book

Written and illustrated by
Jessica Jennings

Dedicated to my
super stars
Katelyn, Zackery,
Charles and Amy.

Aa

is for alligator

**Alligators have
eighty teeth.**

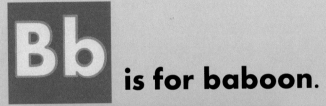

Bb is for baboon.

Baboons travel more than four miles a day.

Cc is for camel

Camels can survive without water for ten months.

Dd is for deer.

Deer can run up to thirty miles per hour.

Ee is for elephant.

Elephants are the world's largest land animal.

Ff is for fox.

There are twelve different fox species in the world.

Gg is for giraffe.

The giraffe neck has the exact same number of bones as a human neck.

Hh is for horse.

Horses can run within hours after birth.

 is for iguana.

Iguanas use visual signals to communicate.

Jj is for jaguar.

Jaguars are the largest feline on the American continent.

Kk is for kangaroo.

Female kangaroos sport a pouch on their belly (made by a fold in the skin) to cradle baby kangaroos, called joeys.

Ll is for leopard.

Leopards spend much of their time high in trees.

Mm is for manatee.

Manatees are also known as the sea cow.

 is for newt.

Newts can grow
lost or damaged
limbs.

Oo is for octopus.

The giant Pacific octopus has three hearts ,nine brains and blue blood.

 **is for parrot.**

Parrots can live for up to one hundred years.

Rr

is for rhinoceros.

Rhinoceros horns are made from keratin..

Ss is for sea lion.

Sea lions use their flippers to walk on land.

Tt is for turtle.

Turtles are reptiles.

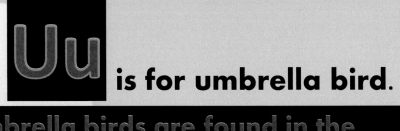

Uu is for umbrella bird.

Umbrella birds are found in the Central and South American rainforests.

 **is for vampire bat**.

Vampire bats have special adaptations to help them with their unique feeding needs.

Ww is for walrus.

Walruses are the gentle giants of the Arctic.

Xx for x-ray fish.

X-ray tetras are notable for having a mostly transparent body.

 **is for yak.**

Yaks live at the highest altitude of any mammal.

Zz is for zebra.

Zebras are constantly on the move for fresh grass to eat and water to drink.

Made in the USA
Middletown, DE
22 November 2019